2007

Mini Saga Competition

Young Writers

in association with

STAEDTLER

mini
S·A·G·A·S·

Derbyshire

First published in Great Britain in 2007 by
Young Writers, Remus House, Coltsfoot Drive,
Peterborough, PE2 9JX
Tel (01733) 890066 Fax (01733) 313524
All Rights Reserved

Disclaimer
Young Writers has maintained every effort
to publish stories that will not cause offence.
Any stories, events or activities relating to individuals
should be read as fictional pieces and not construed
as real-life character portrayal.

Foreword

Young Writers was established in 1991, with the aim of encouraging the children and young adults of today to think and write creatively. Our latest secondary school competition, 'Mini S.A.G.A.S.', posed an exciting challenge for these young authors: to write, in no more than fifty words, a story encompassing a beginning, a middle and an end.
We call this the mini saga.

Mini S.A.G.A.S. Derbyshire is our latest offering from the wealth of young talent that has mastered this incredibly challenging form. With such an abundance of imagination, humour and ability evident in such a wide variety of stories, these young writers cannot fail to enthral and excite with every tale.

Contents

Woodlands Community School

The Mini Sagas

Here I Go Again

Here I go again, running from who knows what,
hoping I can keep on running forever. They say
there's light at the end of the tunnel but I'm not so
sure … maybe running at night wasn't so clever.

Mark Pomroy (15)
Derby Moor Community Sports College

13

They're Watching You . . .

She had a feeling somebody was watching her. This feeling became certainty when, in the darkest corner of the attic, she saw red, glowing eyes. All of a sudden she heard her friend scream with terror and felt a breath on her neck. The goosebumps slowly began to take over …

Effie Gresham (12)
Derby Moor Community Sports College

The Mystery Man

As I woke up on a normal Thursday morning, I
realised it was darker than usual. I looked over to
my window to see a bloodstained man watching me.
I closed, then opened my eyes. He was gone. As I
walked to school I saw him one last time.

Jack Mellors (12)
Derby Moor Community Sports College

Stealthy Assassin

The fighter standing in the shadowed corner, his bionic hand still grasping the hot-barrelled M1 Garnad used to assassinate the king.

'You are surrounded - give yourself up!' bellowed the police.

Beep … boom! The building was destroyed and he was never seen again.

Daniel Vasey (12)
Derby Moor Community Sports College

The Lonely Cottage

Once upon a time there was an old, wrecked, lonely
cottage. A group of kids walked past every day
wondering what was inside.
One day they went in very bravely to see what was
inside. I could hear their voices screaming and then
the door opened but nothing came out.

Jasneet Khaneja (12)
Derby Moor Community Sports College

The Dreadful Day

My first day at school, and what a day it was. I remember the bare corridors, the echo of my footsteps and then *bang!* I sprinted around the corner. There was a little girl. She had a massive gash in her head. After that, all I can remember was screaming.

Holly Earith (12)
Derby Moor Community Sports College

18

Wind . . .

There I was in front of thousands of people, the wind in my hair and the ball under my feet, in control. Just then, I felt the wind through my legs. I had told my mum to get me a smaller size. *'Oh no!'*

Kiran Ditta (12)
Derby Moor Community Sports College

Not Quite An Apocalypse

I was running, not knowing why. Suddenly I smashed straight into a mirror and everything began to spin. It went black. As I opened my eyes and glanced around me, I saw a thick crack running along the ground and realised that half the world had died.

Max Fletcher (12)
Derby Moor Community Sports College

Untitled

One day I was walking to school and my friends were kicking me and poking me all the way. It made me really upset.

When I got to school even the teachers were kicking and poking and the head teacher slapped me. Then someone said, 'Check on your back.'

Joshua Fearon (12)
Derby Moor Community Sports College

The Bad Dream

I woke up and looked in the mirror. I soon realised my hair was gone. I went back to sleep. I woke up, I looked in the mirror … my ears were gone! I went back to sleep. I woke back up … I was looking at a poster. It's a dream.

Brandon Nagra (12)
Derby Moor Community Sports College

Global Warming

A blinding light passes me. Now I see nothing but darkness. The air is too hot, I can't breathe. I'm being swallowed by the water. I can't escape, it's drowning me. Help! This is the future of the human race.

Janiah Rehman (12)
Derby Moor Community Sports College

The House

I saw a house at the end of my street. I went in and I smelt chocolate. I followed the smell, it led me to the wall. I licked the wall, it tasted like chocolate. I ate everything. I came back the next sunny day. There was nothing there.

Adeel Asghar (12)
Derby Moor Community Sports College

24

Here Comes Johnny

I am only six and all my family are dangling from the blossom tree. *Drip, drop,* bloodbath. I can hear their souls screaming, 'Look behind you!' I do. My blood will be all over that wicked tree and I know it. It's time to die. Here comes Johnny …

Simone Swannick (12)
Derby Moor Community Sports College

25

It Was . . .

It was gigantic, it was wide, it was a place where you could hide. It was still, it was alive, it was opening and closing all the time. It was making me scared. I told my mum. She never cared. 'Oh silly billy!' she said … it was only a wardrobe.

Jenaid Ahmed (12)
Derby Moor Community Sports College

Deforestation

I stood and stared. Its fingers clawed at the world around it. Its arms groaned in the wind. Its hair rustled and it stood still. It was talking to me. I went there every day until it had gone. My monster. My best friend ... my tree.

Kershia Field (12)
Derby Moor Community Sports College

27

Drowning?

I try my hardest! I keep sinking. Am I deserted? Is
that the water thrashing against me? I'm going to die!
Am I drowning? Help, help, please someone help!
I cry as I walk out of the swimming baths as usual, I
failed again.

Keisha Manaton (12)
Derby Moor Community Sports College

Crime Tonight . . .

There was crime that night. They were caught but the place was shattered. The cars were trashed, though we weren't. The crime was done but not for the night. That night I stood waiting for my mate to get me home. We didn't manage ... attacked ... we had no chance ...

Jacob Taylor-Durant (12)
Derby Moor Community Sports College

The Game

My heart pumped faster and faster as I approached the ball. At the last second I was fighting to focus as there was shouting in the crowd. I hit the ball with all my might. Would it stay in or go out? Phew, I saw chalk dust.

Ross Trail (11)
Derby Moor Community Sports College

The Penalty Miss

There I was in front of the goal, nervous, the keeper ready to save it. I froze, I didn't know what to do then the manager said, 'Don't be scared, it's only a friendly.'
But then I missed … the manager said, 'Unlucky, better luck next time.'

Elliott Griffiths (12)
Derby Moor Community Sports College

The Haunted House

The wind howled and the moon dimmed, all lights were out apart from his. He couldn't believe he was in a haunted house. He didn't believe in ghosts. Then the doors started creaking. He ran to the front door with his hands in fists, but then he saw the face …

Nikita Mediratta (11)

Derby Moor Community Sports College

32

The Mother's Killer

I was scared, Bubbly was kidnapped. Tanya was going to take him to his mum.
The mother was found dead. The police thought Tanya killed her. Many people were suspected as the murderer but in the end they found out it was the servants. One of the suspects was *me!*

Anisha Hussain (12)
Derby Moor Community Sports College

The Woman

The woman was always walking round school in the darkness at night. I always saw her crying.
I alone was brave enough to investigate. I crept into school and I couldn't believe it. It was actually the head teacher crying about how the school will get knocked down.

Harkiran Bohania (12)
Derby Moor Community Sports College

34

The Man

I was in my soft, comfy hideout. At the big black door there was a man in leather jacket, jeans and Timberlands. He triggered a double-barrelled shotgun alarm with a big loud *bang!* He was no more, so I sneaked over and turned, then the buzzer went at Quaser.

Iain Heaton (12)
Derby Moor Community Sports College

Summer Dreams

Finally summer was here. I went down to Sunset Beach and saw him. We spoke and had a great time. He took me on a date, I loved every minute. I went to his house. We kissed then … *boom!* My mum woke me up for school. What a great dream.

Lomara McDonald (12)
Derby Moor Community Sports College

The Dare

'Anila, your turn.'

My face went red as Anisha told me to do it. I had to do it otherwise people would call me things.

I went as slowly as I could. Tiptoeing, trying not to get scared, I went to the teacher and then, 'Can I go toilet?' I said.

Anila Abis (12)

Derby Moor Community Sports College

37

The Lucky 7s

A gang known as the Lucky 7s met up. They all saw and heard someone screaming. They tried to see what was going on. While they were running through the forest they heard tree branches breaking and saw animals in a stampede. When they got there, a man was dead.

Adif Nawaz (14)
Derby Moor Community Sports College

38

William And His Politically Correct Public

I am awesome. You look upon me; frown, or desperately try to avoid eye contact. Whatever, I pity you rats, you 'PC' rats. I am free, below your eye level. I am free. Freedom weaves through even the holes of my grimy blanket. I am awesome, free. Spare change, please.

Jasmine Bertie (15)

Derby Moor Community Sports College

Nightmare

'One … two … three …'
'Go away, please!' she cried sadly. Frozen solid
with fear, she hid behind her blanket; isolated. One
monster after another flashed before her eyes. Her
last hope was to clamber across the wilderness
and turn on her light. She glanced behind as they
disintegrated before her eyes.

Class 10Y
Derby Moor Community Sports College

Silent Stalker

'Help! Help me, please!' she screamed. Her breathing was snatched and irregular. Her heart was kicking in her chest. She clutched her leg in pain. Blood spilled over her hands. He came again, and stood near her. In his hand was the bloody knife. He plunged it brutally in her …

Salma Suboor (13)
Derby Moor Community Sports College

41

Electric

I've been anticipating this night for weeks. I was honoured, privileged, to be one of the lucky few with tickets. Queueing was painful. I couldn't wait another minute. The place was buzzing and the atmosphere was electric. The lights dimmed and the crowd roared. We sat in the dark, waiting.

Alec Curtis (15)
Derby Moor Community Sports College

Mint?

Happy faces – lovely aren't they? I walk through this crowded place with a spring in my step. I giggle. Good times! I ask the people around me if they would like to indulge in a mint? I get funny looks. I guess these people aren't as cool as I thought.

Rachel Short (15)
Derby Moor Community Sports College

No More

Two figures lay in the long grass, fighting. Minutes passed by, they were exhausted. One stirred the grass – slipping, she got up. Red as she yanked it out. He was dead. She broke down, cried. Revenge, anger and hate left her. The sun rose in the ethereal dawn.

Jonathan Plunkett (15)
Derby Moor Community Sports College

44

The Emergency

The day had begun. *Beep!* He had missed the flight.
The next flight was 9.30pm. 'I can't wait that long!'
He booked a flight with another airline. He got on
the plane then suddenly the phone rang.
'It's alright, you don't need to come now, I'm fine!'
his daughter explained.

Kirsty Reeves (11)
Derby Moor Community Sports College

45

School!

There was a girl named Holly. She couldn't stand school so she decided to forge a doctor's note. She had the whole day off! But then her parents found out. They said, 'You don't need a doctor's note on Saturday.'

Amy Frith (11)

Derby Moor Community Sports College

46

Mountain

His fingers were raw and cold. Each grip was more painful than the last. Jack couldn't see a thing, the snow was too heavy. The view was now a cloudy mist. He knew he had to keep going though, the cave was right above. He smiled as he reached it.

Camilla White (11)
Derby Moor Community Sports College

47

The New Girl

'Morning, everyone,' said the teacher. 'We have a new girl, her name's Lauren, so can we have a volunteer to take her around the school?'
'I will,' said Lorine.
'Thank you, Lorine.'
It became the end of the day. We were best friends forever and we never, ever had fights.

Lorine Wint (12)
Derby Moor Community Sports College

48

Night At The Movies

I walked in, popcorn in my hand. The room was pitch-black. I kept walking right to the front.
'Shush, the movie's started.'
I started walking faster so I didn't miss anything. I walked into the row of seats, sat down and zzzzz. Oh great, not another one! Damn!

Sam Chambers (12)
Derby Moor Community Sports College

The Night They Took Him

Pain shot through his legs. He recounted the events from before, walking down the dark streets, ignoring youths on the street corner. He was going home for the night. They had other plans. Two steps later he was on the ground, bundled into a van. They had come for him.

Remi Warren (15)
Derby Moor Community Sports College

Last Resort

Splash! One by one each tear fell to the floor.
Depressed, lonely. *What shall I do?* Thoughts flew
through her head. One thing was certain. Scared.
Petrified. Wind blew through her hair, her fingers
clutched the pendant. 'Last chance,' she whispered.
Waves crashed on the cliff. Last breath. Jump.

Laura Mills (15)
Derby Moor Community Sports College

51

Choppy

Rocking sideways rapidly, my head spinning, my heart racing. The sea was choppy. The crew were not scared one bit. Only me. Thunder appeared until the sea lay still. *One extreme to another,* I thought. Peaceful now, no more worries. The boat drifted into an iceberg. *Crash!* The boat sank.

Alicia Cliffe (15)

Derby Moor Community Sports College

Cruel

One nice sunny day I was walking through a forest. I heard a noise. What was it? It sounded like a trapped fox, so I ran to see if I could help. I was right, it was a fox trapped by a metal trap. Why are people so cruel?

Daniel Taylor (11)
Dronfield Henry Fanshawe School

Untitled

One damp and warm day, tumbling through the rainforest, me and my best mate climbing, then suddenly there it was, glistening in the sun. It was difficult to reach because there were branches and twisted vines and leaves. Was it a ring? No, it was a piece of glass.

Jake Parkin (12)
Dronfield Henry Fanshawe School

Out Of My Window

When I look out of my window, I see a swooping creature. It cuts through the sky like a knife through butter, then *zoom* comes a speeding car. The bird jumps for safety from the zooming vehicle. Next, it swoops down to catch its evening meal to feed its young.

Moffie Littlewood (12)

Dronfield Henry Fanshawe School

Old Trees Have Weird Things In Them

Me and my friend, Emma, were climbing the old tree in my garden. It's really big and broad. Emma climbed ahead. I heard her scream. I gripped the tree. I heard her shout, 'I've slid and broken something.' Emma was on the floor, several pieces of slide scattered around her.

Rebecca Bierton (12)
Dronfield Henry Fanshawe School

Shining Beach

I was on a beach sitting down when I saw something shining bright, so I walked down the beach. Getting nearer to the sea I couldn't see anything but I carried on walking. As I got closer, it got hotter, then I peeked round. There was nothing but total silence.

Brittany Holmes (11)
Dronfield Henry Fanshawe School

Horror Night

Screaming, roaring. Downstairs, horrifying noises. I got my chainsaw from my cupboard. I was going downstairs and then the noises suddenly started getting fizzy-sounding and worse. Then I saw the tape recorder. My brothers were probably trying to annoy me. Then I turned around. My mum jumped suddenly, *'Boo!'*

Matthew Conway (12)
Dronfield Henry Fanshawe School

Alone

The wind blowing through my hair, the sea crawling along the shore, I could feel the sand between my toes, the sun beaming down on me. I could feel a bitter wind coming in my direction. I suddenly disappeared in the gloomy fog with only my footsteps to trace me!

Christie Bell (12)
Dronfield Henry Fanshawe School

Zodiac

A car rolls silently towards his victim. The gong of death rings. Police baffled and no clues. The familiar sign shows. Country on red alert and all over the news. He's back. Zodiac. Beware.

Jake Bingham (13)
Dronfield Henry Fanshawe School

Sleepwalk

Up at night late, wandering in the house. It's chilly,
I feel it down my spine. Feet won't go in the right
direction. I stop, shake, tremble with fear. A ghost
looks like me. I pass on, back to the comfort of bed.

Amie Smith (13)
Dronfield Henry Fanshawe School

Space School

It was a normal day, maths, spelling etc. My teacher scratched her face, revealing scales. I ran to the head, only to find a bloodsucking alien there. As I jumped through the window, school was in space. As gunge filled my nostrils, scales replaced the skin on my neck.

Chris Shipley (12)

Dronfield Henry Fanshawe School

Untitled

I walked through the doors but I was bewildered when I found I was standing on a cliff. Suddenly, a huge mythical beast blundered by while it let out a thunderous roar. It was a griffin, so I walked back out. I was at school, a mythical realm, alone. Strange!

William North (12)
Dronfield Henry Fanshawe School

Fake Money

I was walking through town by myself when I spotted it there, a twenty-pound note just lying on the floor. I walked towards it slowly, bent down, went to grab it but I couldn't grab it and everyone started laughing. Then I realised it was painted on the floor.

Holly Fairclough (12)
Dronfield Henry Fanshawe School

The Killer Lollipop!

'Mmm!' said the girl as she licked the sugar-filled lollipop. 'This is tasty,' said the girl, licking her lips like a dog. But suddenly she fell to the floor. 'Help!' she cried. No one came, so she died on the spot with the lolly stuck to her lips suspiciously!

Suzannah Curry (12)
Dronfield Henry Fanshawe School

The Jump

I walked through the town. It was crowded. I ran
to see what was happening. Then I saw. Police,
ambulances, fire brigade. Was he crazy? They were
shouting at him, wanting no one to get hurt. It was
getting late but I couldn't stop watching. I waited.
Then he jumped …

Amber Coates (11)
Dronfield Henry Fanshawe School

What Was That?

I was reading in my room when I heard a sound, a small creak. There it was again. Then I realised it was footsteps and they were heading for my door. Shock, horror hit me. Where would I go? Who would I tell? The door slammed open and then …

Alex Glossop (12)
Dronfield Henry Fanshawe School

Untitled

It was a normal day, taking my dog for a walk. Everything was quiet. I heard some footsteps coming towards me. I turned around. A man with an axe was staring right at me. I ran as fast as I could; he chased after me. I died that night.

Grace Coulson (11)
Dronfield Henry Fanshawe School

Vampire

Down the street I walked, smashed a window and entered the house. I searched the house from head to toe to find my food. As I found my prize, my mouth watered. Finally, after a long night I sank my teeth into a nice big ... carrot!

Sophie Whitfield (12)
Dronfield Henry Fanshawe School

Beauty Is A Chore

My world-depressing clouds over my head, I needed
to be beautiful. That night's dream seemed so real.
I was popular, beautiful, in love. Dreams became
nightmares, I awoke in cold sweats. I realised beauty
is a chore. I'm not as vain as that. My desire for
beauty … gone.

Abigail Clark (13)
Dronfield Henry Fanshawe School

70

Madness

They're mad! I thought, saying that Dracula was real.
Completely bonkers, madness, until that day, that
night. I was in bed. I woke up. I heard something.
What was that? I rubbed my eyes. It couldn't be; he
didn't exist! I looked again. *Argh!* I'm a vampire now.

Mark Simmonite (12)
Dronfield Henry Fanshawe School

School

I dread school, I always do. I don't want to go. It's
not my fault I'm lonely and unpopular.
I walked out the house and down the road. I saw her,
the big bully. I went up to her and thumped her one.
She cried. She's not so tough now.

Naomi Smith (12)
Dronfield Henry Fanshawe School

Be Careful Before You Wish

I was a human before now, but now I'm a bird. It all started in an overgrown forest when I saw a well. I wished I was a bird and now I fly from tree to tree, trying not to be eaten by predators. So be careful before you wish.

Mathew Sanderson (12)
Dronfield Henry Fanshawe School

The Stranger At The Door

There was a knock at the door, I thought it would be a friend. I opened the door to find a tall man wearing all black. I didn't recognise him, he wasn't from around here. He looked very strange. He had mysterious eyes and twitchy lips. That night, I died!

Georgina Warrington (12)
Dronfield Henry Fanshawe School

Just Like That

I was breathing heavily, my back stuck against the wall, my heart pounding like a drum in the dark. I knew he was there, he had been for a few weeks; waiting, still, no movement, I do not know what for. Suddenly he disappeared without a trace, just like that.

Laura Siddall (12)
Dronfield Henry Fanshawe School

The Man At The Gate

I woke up and went straight to the kitchen. As I went to the sink, I looked out of the window because something caught my eye. There was a knock, I went to answer, no one was there. I went back and the man was stood by the sink, staring.

Charlotte Walker (12)
Dronfield Henry Fanshawe School

Zombies

I woke up one morning and walked down the road.
There were these weird looking things on the other
side of the road. I looked more closely, they were
zombies! These zombie creatures were everywhere.
Every human being they saw died as soon as the
zombies touched them.

Louise Mather (12)
Dronfield Henry Fanshawe School

What Happens In The Kitchens

New dinner ladies started at our school today.
Bubbling, boiling, salt, pepper and the evil dinner
ladies' cackle. They add some dishwater in the
casserole and some toilet water in the cheese sauce.
Little Billy had his dinner. It tasted different. 'Mmm!'
he said, and went for more cheese sauce.

Joanna Channon (12)
Dronfield Henry Fanshawe School

Faint Lights

It was dark with only a few faint lights. I heard
someone coming. They shot me and I shot them
back. My gun ran out so I filled it up again. The
lights came on, the game had finished. I loved it at
Lazerzone. I want to go again sometime.

Hannah Walker (12)
Dronfield Henry Fanshawe School

79

Here We Go Again!

Over the hill we went, faster and faster until we came to a sudden halt. Barbie and Ken were crossing the road. I burst into laughter, thinking of when I used to play with my Barbie. We carried on until we found ourselves in Barbie Land. It was extremely wonderful.

Lucy Vaughan (12)
Dronfield Henry Fanshawe School

Is This Real Or Just TV?

They came closer. Blue lights everywhere, ice-blue lights. Gold-plated bodies. Cruel war cries erupting everywhere. Screams everywhere. Bright white beams everywhere. I ran. I ran as far as possible. The gold things behind me were screaming, 'Halt or you will be exterminated.'

Gonner, I thought. Doctor Who finished.

Matt Cross (13)
Dronfield Henry Fanshawe School

Watching Angel

She sat beside me holding my shoulders like I was about to break. 'Don't worry, I've heard living in Heaven is beautiful,' she sobbed. I drew my last ragged breath and died in 1916. From that day on I have watched over Isabella, making sure her shoulders will never break.

Philippa Kartawick (13)

Dronfield Henry Fanshawe School

Time Lord

As the blue rays of light go through my head, I see the start and the end of everything. As time passes, I do not age. Although I'm as old as time and still looking young. I have been places where you do not know of. I'm a Time Lord.

Glen Gregory (12)
Dronfield Henry Fanshawe School

The Black Cat

In the woods, very dark, a black cat following the girl, her parents and grandma. Screaming from her mum … screaming from her dad … screaming from her gran. The girl turned … her family dead. She woke up hearing screaming … a black cat at the bottom of her bed, pounding towards her.

Hannah Gregory (13)
Dronfield Henry Fanshawe School

My First Day At School

I got to school, got out my stationery, rulers - check! Pencils - check! Rubbers - check! But … oh no! I had lost my pen! I searched everywhere: my bag, the classroom, the playground, but I could not find it. I got home later. There it was, on the kitchen table. Silly me!

Megan Yapp (12)
Dronfield Henry Fanshawe School

Obedience

The sun arose from outside the window. I sat waiting on a rickety chair. Before I knew it, my mouth was forced open and books and pencils were pushed to the back of my throat. I was lifted into the cold air and then carried out into the real world.

Sophie Newton (13)
Dronfield Henry Fanshawe School

Captain Bark Wolf

'Leagueship closing in!' bellowed the Oakelf.
Captain Lawrenson, known as Barkwolf, answered,
'Lower the mainsail!'
'Leagueship boarding,' cried a sky-pirate.
'Attack!' cried Barkwolf.
The sky-pirates jumped into action. *Slash! Crash!*
Bang! The sky-pirates won with no casualties.
'Hooray!' cheered the sky-pirates. Then out of the
void, a hundred leagueships appeared!

Gabriel Wilson (11)
Dronfield Henry Fanshawe School

Crash!

One day I was driving along a particularly busy road. Although it was my usual route to work, it seemed different. Suddenly, a stupid boy ran out into the road. *Crash!* Had I hit him? Thank goodness, no! I had swerved in time, but my car was in a tree!

Brontë Effin (12)
Dronfield Henry Fanshawe School

Highwayman Waiting

On a dark road due south, I sit on my horse waiting for travellers. With my rapier and gun I steal their possessions. I sell them to a trader or a smith. I use the money to buy new weapons, ammo, food and drink. I'm thought of as a criminal.

Christopher Preece (13)
Dronfield Henry Fanshawe School

Specimen

I stared at the specimen and stared and it got closer and closer. A blinding light came from nowhere and the rumble of a monster truck landing a jump filled the air. It was a truck coming towards me.

David Coffier (13)
Dronfield Henry Fanshawe School

Jolene's Noises

Every night Jolene wakes up to a strange noise. It's a kind of squeaky laugh, more like a high-pitched scream. She shakes and eventually falls back to sleep. As the noise fades she wonders what it is worrying and scaring her each night, but it's only the washing machine.

Philippa Allen (13)
Dronfield Henry Fanshawe School

91

Demon Teacher

'No, Sir, I didn't do it, I swear!' I said fearfully.
'It's too late for you David, your time is up.'
'But Sir, I really didn't do it. Really, it wasn't me.'
'Oh, so plead your case, Mr David. Plead your case.'
'No! I didn't do my homework. Stop shouting!'

Daniel Coates (13)
Dronfield Henry Fanshawe School

The Time-Stopping Hole

It was a beautiful sunny day and five children went out to play hide-and-seek in a field. Two of the children fell down a hole. They followed the hole and saw many mythical beasts. When they got out of the hole, Jack was still counting.

Sam Cook (13)
Dronfield Henry Fanshawe School

BMX Trick

Travelling at high speeds along the murky dirt track, as I went up the muddy ramp I got really good height. As I landed the jump, a rock obstructed my path. *Smack* went my defenceless body to the dirty ground. As the pain increased, a dark shadow leered over me.

Adam Lee (13)
Dronfield Henry Fanshawe School

Caving Curiosity

It was a hot summer's day, the sun was beaming down on the golden bay. Three girls walked along the side of the rocks. They came to a cave and gazed inside. There was something gleaming in the light of the sun. It was on a rock, the glistening diamond.

Aimée Harrison (13)
Dronfield Henry Fanshawe School

If I Were A Butterfly

If I were a butterfly I would fluttery by each and every flower, catching people's eyes with my pretty power, flying extremely high, getting lost in the glittering sky. I'd go to sleep, rest my wings, wondering what tomorrow brings. This would be my life if I were a butterfly.

Hope Parkin (13)
Dronfield Henry Fanshawe School

Fort Dragonblood

Where dragons fly high and blood turns blue,
the legend of Fort Dragonblood awaits. A young
adventurer looked at the huge shadow plummeting
towards him. He drew his bow and let an arrow fly.
Blood sprayed everywhere; the dragon turned to
stone. That is the legend of Fort Dragonblood.

Ashley Pearson (13)
Dronfield Henry Fanshawe School

97

Banging On The Door

I woke up and heard a noise. I looked out of the window and there were people outside. They had masks on. One started to walk towards the house. He rang the bell and looked up. He saw me. I opened the door and then … 'Trick or treat?'

Calvin Harris (13)
Dronfield Henry Fanshawe School

Bounce Me

The boy kept picking me up and throwing me on the floor. Suddenly, he put me back in a box. I was surrounded by lots of other things that looked similar to me. Then a girl took one of us out of the box.

Alex Hadfield (13)
Dronfield Henry Fanshawe School

The Closet

I sit in the cold, dark space, waiting for someone to come and find me. I can feel the others around me; they are waiting too. I suddenly hear footsteps entering the room. Doors fling open and I am slipped on some feet and carried away. I'm put back later.

Rebecca Jeffery (13)
Dronfield Henry Fanshawe School

Rapunzel

Rapunzel was skipping through the woods one day when the Three Bears chased her. Rapunzel ran to the gingerbread man's house and hid in a giant cookie jar. The Three Bears went away and ate fairy cakes, so Rapunzel went to Cinderella's gigantic house and lived happily ever after.

Kerry Whelpton (13)
Dronfield Henry Fanshawe School

The Big Pond

I'm in a massive pond. I used to be a lot bigger than
I am now and had rough edges. But because I get
pushed and brushed along the bed past all my friends,
I am smooth. The other day I got pushed out of the
water onto the sand.

Lewis Delahay-Johnson (13)
Dronfield Henry Fanshawe School

The Forgotten Shelf

Here I sit, looking down on everyone from my dusty shelf. I hate it here. Nobody cares about me anymore; all memories of me forgotten. One day they might remember me. I see them with all the others. One day they will end up like me. Just a forgotten toy.

Bryony Smith (13)
Dronfield Henry Fanshawe School

The Tennis Ball

Plastic hits my body, I fall onto the concrete. I fly back up into the air. I'm falling again and I hit the floor, the hard stone pushes me back into the air. I'm flying at great speed. I hit the net and fall down to the ground. Henman wins.

Ben Dyson (13)
Dronfield Henry Fanshawe School

What Am I?

One day I was with the others, until a man came and started peeling off my skin with a knife. He took all of my pieces apart. It was painful. After, he picked me up and put me somewhere I haven't been before. It looked like a cage to me.

Adam Tiffer (13)
Dronfield Henry Fanshawe School

Eggs

One day I went to the shop to buy lots of eggs. I hated the teacher, so I was going to egg his house. When I arrived he was outside, so I got out all my eggs and threw them at his head. I felt much better. He didn't.

Daniel Goodall (13)

Dronfield Henry Fanshawe School

Panic Attack

One winter's day I was walking through a white field.
Suddenly, I saw a black figure on the floor. I started
running towards the figure, flapping my arms to scare
the birds away. Sweat was dripping from my face. I
got there and it was a stuffed man of straw.

Harvey Torr (12)
Dronfield Henry Fanshawe School

The Unexpected Driver

I was walking to school yesterday, when a man pulled up his car next to me. He told me to get in the car. I started running, flapping my arms frantically. I fell and was rolling down the hill, when I turned around to realise he wasn't talking to me.

Mark Smith (12)
Dronfield Henry Fanshawe School

Untitled

The fire was burning as I dived through the smoke. I shot as blood covered my face. He'd been shot from head to toe, his blood covering me, rage overcoming my confused mind. I was pushed to the very limit as I killed the assassin. I knew it was over.

CJ Cooper (13)
Dronfield Henry Fanshawe School

Run!

The wind and rain hammered against him but still he carried on. Oscar loved to run, whatever the weather, whatever the time. He sprinted round the corner and, through blurred eyes, he saw the bullies at the school gate. He wanted to run and at that point … he did.

Joanne Muntus (13)
Dronfield Henry Fanshawe School

Alone And Afraid

'Mother!' the girl shouted again. Still no answer. She was alone and cold. Slowly and shivering, she stood up and looked around. *Whoosh,* the sudden blowing of leaves and snapping twigs signaled to her that she wasn't alone after all. 'Mother!' she shouted again, but louder. She was now afraid.

Amy Vickers (13)
Dronfield Henry Fanshawe School

Parachute

I floated down. For some reason a man gripped my legs, pulling and yanking like I was some sort of object without thoughts or feelings. We got to the floor and my body crashed down, lifeless, until I was stuffed back in the backpack to leap from the plane again.

Jack Brown (12)

Dronfield Henry Fanshawe School

Cattack!

Suddenly he realised something was wrong. His eyes began to twitch and the constant sneezing was becoming unbearable. It jumped on him. It was soft and fluffy but its claws stuck into his trousers like pins. 'Ow!' he yelped. It clung on tightly. He stood up and screamed, 'Stupid cat!'

Kirsten Emery (13)
Dronfield Henry Fanshawe School

Too Late

Shannon and I were playing in the countryside. Suddenly I heard a faint buzzing sound. I told Shannon to pack up because I thought a tractor was coming. It came into sight: a crash-landing aeroplane coming straight for us! We ran! It was too late … I'll never forget Shannon.

Bethany Holland (12)
Dronfield Henry Fanshawe School

Footsteps

I was at the park when I heard a noise; footsteps following me. I headed for the woods. The footsteps got quicker. I panicked, ran further into the woods, then I was lost. The footsteps stopped and a man appeared. he put his hand in his pocket … my mobile! Hooray!

Shannon Holland (12)
Dronfield Henry Fanshawe School

A Man And Saint Peter

A guy was stuck on a roof. A helicopter and two boats came to rescue him. He said, 'No, the Lord will save me.' He drowned.
At Heaven's gates he met Saint Peter. He asked, 'Why didn't you save me?'
He replied, 'I sent two boats, a helicopter. What else?'

Sebastian Friedmann (11)
Dronfield Henry Fanshawe School

The Garage

It was a bright summer's day. I was riding my bike when I caught a glimpse of a red fluid seeping from under the garage door. Groans of agony came from the room. A man appeared, covered in the red fluid, and asked, 'Do you know how to paint, please?'

Chris Wright (12)
Dronfield Henry Fanshawe School

The Bike Ride

Me and my brother, Andy, were racing. We saw the sign saying *Slow Down*. I stopped; my brother continued at thirty miles per hour. He skidded down the hill. He was bruised, scraped, grazed, one black eye, no two. He broke an arm and a leg. 'You OK?' I asked.

Matthew Bean (12)
Dronfield Henry Fanshawe School

A Fatal Blow

A fatal blow to the chest and I fell to the ground.
People's laughter merged together and my vision
became impaired. I was bleeding internally and drops
of liquid landed heavily on the grass. I leapt to my
feet, saturated and grinning, and squirted them all!
Water fights are fun!

Megan Hobson (13)
Dronfield Henry Fanshawe School

Run!

I shuddered until I was scared. I was scared until I
was worried. I was worried until I was frightened. I
was frightened until I fell into a fit of giggles. I never
knew that pranks were so obvious, until I realised
this wasn't another prank. This was real. Run!

Chloe Cheetham (13)
Dronfield Henry Fanshawe School

Goldfish Bowl

'I wonder what's on the other side of this bowl?'
Over the treasure chest, under the bridge, through
the plastic reeds and into my castle. I come out again,
five second memory span … gone. 'Hmm, I wonder
what's on the other side of this bowl?'

Jessica Street (11)
Dronfield Henry Fanshawe School

The Mystery Ship

Walking alone down the silent beach when suddenly, out of the mist came a ship that got closer till it hit the edge of the sand. I was frozen. From the ship came screeching noises. Very wisely, I ran. After a while I eagerly went back. The ship had gone.

Shauna Holland (12)
Dronfield Henry Fanshawe School

In The Darkness

My heart pounds as my friend hits the ground,
his killer stepping towards me, as if an angry bull
ready to get us. Up comes his gun. In the deafening
silence and the eerie darkness I am cornered, his
gun pointing to my chest. But then again, it's only
Lazerzone.

Eleanor Ashton (12)
Dronfield Henry Fanshawe School

Music

Music, a mind-blowing interest. Different beats, rhythms and sounds. Lyrics that tell many stories, through powerful sounds and words. Some songs fast and hard to understand, others slow, emotional and depressing to listen to. So many different bands battling each other for fame, while others just enjoy making music.

Georgina Birtles (12)
Dronfield Henry Fanshawe School

Good Luck

There was a boy called Jeff. He was on his way to school but he stepped in a muddy puddle. He didn't get wet. He carried on walking then he fell over but he didn't hurt himself. Then he crossed the road and got run over by a bus.

Jessica Stacey (12)
Dronfield Henry Fanshawe School

The True Story

Jack and Jill went up the hill to fetch a pail of cider. Jill got drunk and gave Jack a thump, so Jack rolled down and laid there. Jack sued Jill in court and claimed for compensation. Jill coughed up the money. The judge started a beautiful relationship with Jack.

Mylo Charlesworth (12)
Dronfield Henry Fanshawe School

Sailing

The waves were tumbling over us. 'Man overboard,'
he shouted. The life ring was thrown over the deck.
We dragged him back on board. The waves were
getting higher.
'Bring the sails down!' Captain shouted.
I leaned over the side of the boat …
'Finished in the bath?' Mum asked.

Isobel Jones (12)
Dronfield Henry Fanshawe School

Wrong Washer

Mini Louise was in her bedroom too long.
'Louise, we're going to get coffee!' I shouted. No reply. I knocked again … no reply. 'Louise … are you OK?' I asked.
She peeked out from behind the door. 'I washed my trousers and they shrank!'
'This is why we don't wash clothes!'

Hoffy Pfatts (12)
Dronfield Henry Fanshawe School

128

Owl

Ask me how I cope, ask me how I survive trapped in these woods with nowhere to go. Plenty of fruit, ripe and tasty. No one likes the darkness, but darkness is my friend. At night I hunt and sweep down low. My prey is petrified. They're such stupid suckers!

Oliver Barrett (12)
Dronfield Henry Fanshawe School

Mary's Little Lamb

Mary had a little lamb who followed her everywhere.
She kept it on a little lead and everyone would stare.
One day she let go, frightened by a toad. The lamb
was hit by a speeding car in the nearby road. Mary
refused to cry. She bought a new one.

Lauren Sharpe (12)
Dronfield Henry Fanshawe School

Hallowe'en

Hallowe'en night, the doorbell chimed. 'I've got it,
Dad.' (There was no answer.) I opened the door,
a masked man said, 'Come with me child, you're
mine.'
Frantically I tried to get away but he dragged me into
the corner and said, 'Do you like my costume, son?'

Matthew Weston (12)
Dronfield Henry Fanshawe School

Alien

'Help!'
Blood was spitting out of its mouth, drooling saliva all over.
'Argh! Let go of my leg.'
Crack! Blood was spilling out of my leg as the dinosaur ripped it out of its socket.
'Ben, stop playing with that fake blood and your alien toy. You're making a racket.'

Joe Johnson (12)
Dronfield Henry Fanshawe School

The Swimming Trip

I was on the bus going to the sports centre to have a swimming lesson. I got changed and ran in. My friend pushed me into the swimming pool. I swam around, I felt cold. I looked down, my shorts had fallen off! I shouted out very, very loudly, *'No!'*

Nasser Fahad (12)
Dronfield Henry Fanshawe School

Champions League

I was getting ready for the big football match, the Champions League final in Athens. We had to set off early to get to the airport. We were late for the plane. We got the next flight. Eventually we arrived. We ended up in the wrong place. Disaster, disaster, disaster!

Lewis Atkinson (12)
Dronfield Henry Fanshawe School

Plane Crash

The plane ripped across the sky. Fire swept the wings. I felt helpless as the mighty crash suddenly shook us all as the plane skidded over the rough ground. There was another loud boom, almost deafening, followed by a loud silence. Then I got off the fairground simulator.

Christopher Arbon (12)
Dronfield Henry Fanshawe School

Mary Had
A Piece Of Lamb

Mary had a piece of lamb that she bought from the
market and everywhere that Mary went, the lamb
was in the basket. She brought it home to eat for tea
but Granny looked a bit hairy. Granny was a wolf that
ate the delicious lamb and poor young Mary.

Katherine Saunders (12)
Dronfield Henry Fanshawe School

The Fifty-Word Container

I was out in the garden digging with my shovel. When I placed it in the ground, I heard the sound of metal, *whoooo!* There's a metal container in the ground. I wondered what it was? Gold, or maybe a bomb? Shaking, I opened the metal lid. There was nothingness.

Oliver Ashton (12)
Dronfield Henry Fanshawe School

Phew!

'Argh!' There a figure stood still in Charles' bedroom. The fear rushed through him as he clutched onto his bed. The figure didn't move, just stood still. You could just make out the long hair and skinny body then, 'Argh!' The light shone. 'Mum?' he called. 'Oh phew,' he whispered.

Effe Cundy (12)
Dronfield Henry Fanshawe School

Humpty Dumpty

Hi, I'm Humpty Dumpty. I tried to climb a wall but then I fell. Have you ever tried that? Don't, it's really hard. Anyway, all the king's horses and all the king's men couldn't put me together again. Now I don't climb walls, I just walk past them.

Helen Connor (12)
Dronfield Henry Fanshawe School

A Magical Land

I was walking along a path in the park, searching for the loud noise of happy children laughing and screaming. I carried on walking and climbed through bushes and saw a magical land. A child came to me and said, 'Don't get too over-excited, it is only a park!'

Rebecca Smith (12)
Dronfield Henry Fanshawe School

The Shock At The Beach

One summer, I was swimming in the sea when something bit me. I went underwater to see what it was and a giant fish swam away. I looked down and a huge red crab nipped me again. I ran out of the sea and put ice on my foot.

Emily Gordon (12)
Dronfield Henry Fanshawe School

Arctic Wolf

Stealthily I creep, treading through the white snow, peering through the dense brown trees, searching for a tasty meal. A gunshot fires. I lie in wait until the hunter moves on. Jump and bounce, leap and pounce, running through the woods, finding food to feed my family of wolves.

Holly Scothern (12)
Dronfield Henry Fanshawe School

Football Match

On a hot summer's day, me and my friend were playing footy. I shot, I scored in the top corner. It was unbelievable. The keeper had no chance. I was 1-0 up. The game finished. We won the final, it was amazing. We were the winners of the cup.

Jack Lambert (12)
Dronfield Henry Fanshawe School

That Flushed Feeling

I'm begging for energy and adrenaline as I'm chasing for oxygen, my blood is rushing. My feet skidding across the ground, my face pale, the pain excruciating. My sweat making puddles on the cold, rigid ground as I scream in agony. Then finally, finished. I sigh in glory and flush.

Joshua Clark (12)
Dronfield Henry Fanshawe School

Prospero's Past

Seven years ago in Milan there was a great duke called Prospero. His treacherous brother, called Antonio, plotted with King Alonso to overthrow Duke Prospero. A large group of soldiers charged the duke's home. Prospero was taken to the king, who banished the duke and his family. They sailed away.

Joe Traif (12)
Landau Forte College

Storm

The ship swayed in the wind, side to side as if it was
a gentle pond. The journey was going very well, the
captain was pleased with the progress made.
'Sir, we've spotted a man,' said a crewman.
Suddenly, a storm sank the ship at a nearby beach.
Few survived.

Hayden Shaw (13)
Landau Forte College

It!

I'm an it. Nothing but an it. Treated like dirt, a piece of scrap! I have to do things for my master: his duties, his wants, his needs, making things go wrong. With our magic he does anything. I just want to be free, being who I want to be!

Chelsey Drakeley (13)
Landau Forte College

First Love

He saw her. She saw him. They gazed into each other's eyes. They fell for each other. But her father hated him. They stuck together through hatred. The father saw this, had a change of heart, all was forgiven. The father gave his blessing and they would soon be wed.

Tanzela Hussain (13)
Landau Forte College

Love Across The Water

Windy, lonely island. All on my own, no friends, just some creatures, my father and me. I finally find love. I'm happy, too happy. Now I'm sad. My father said no. Lost, sad and lonely again. He returns. My father thinks deeply, he agrees. We live happily ever after.

Ankush Kumar (13)
Landau Forte College

My Love

I saw him for the first time, my heart sank. Every time he spoke his words would send me to Heaven. Our love is like a rainbow, you can never see the end. Father disapproves of my prince but love manages to shine through. It's my fairy-tale ending!

Hoffy Beffamy (13)
Landau Forte College

Another Innocent Life

OK, I will let you go while you're driving, love y … !
(Phone goes dead.) His signal must have gone.
Later on that evening …
'Tonight on BBC News, young man killed in a car
crash while on the phone to his girlfriend. Another
innocent life taken, and what for?'

Katya Kasyta-Jubb (13)
Landau Forte College

Silence

I was running, enjoying the fresh breeze against my face. My ankle buckled and I tumbled down the filthy bank. My hand broke the river's film; I began to slide, grappling onto the sludge. I was too weak again. My last emotion was mindless panic. No one could hear me.

Sarah-Jessica Lewis (15)
Landau Forte College

Untitled

Someone driving in a car, a bright light shines from behind him and smashes straight into eight bollards and into a tree. The car was taken straight to the scrapyard. He lost his car and gained a body cast.

Natalie Grace (16)
Landau Forte College

What Happened?

At school he was uncertain; a low-grader. Me? I was confident – straight As. Help him? Why? Twenty years later he is happy and popular; his family so proud; well known for charity work. Me? I feel depressed and lonely as I sit silently in my luxurious, spacious, beautiful mansion.

Kalisha Hamilton (15)
Landau Forte College

A Landscape

Clouds swirl overhead, their eddies catching the sun's light as I watch. The wind blows stronger. The darkness gathers and pools of shadow form: blocking out the sun that was so bright. Lightning flashes in the air and thunder peals across the turbulent plain. My heart tremors, then is still.

Christopher Arran (15)
Landau Forte College

The Runaway Car

He started the car. Suddenly he remembered he had forgotten his laptop. He left the car with the engine running. He returned, he pulled the handle on the door. It was locked. Peering through the window he could see the keys. All of a sudden, the car drove off.

James Blount (15)
Landau Forte College

My Horse

The pain was unbearable. I will never forget what happened. Something so special to me, something I was so proud of, caused me this pain. I cried in fear as I saw it approaching me again. My horse ran over my limp body. 'Why has this happened?' I screamed.

Kayleigh Johnson (15)
Landau Forte College

The Scream

The scream echoed through the mountains. It travelled far from its origin, a small clearing in the forest. The young girl stood there astounded, shocked, terrified, frozen. Her eyes fixed to that one point, that one image, the image that would haunt her for the rest of her life.

Hayley Millar (15)
Landau Forte College

The Robbery

Walking to school one day, listening to my MP3 player, I saw a man running out of a shop. He knocked me flying, so I chased after him. I managed to knock him down with my bag. Two minutes later the cops arrived. They said I was a hero.

Sam Reid (15)
Landau Forte College

For Eternity

The excruciating pain lasting for seconds; seems like eternity. My body changing, becoming one of them. There's incisions on my body in groups of two. Lifeless, my body lays with the dark shadows feeding on my life to give me another to lead for eternity.

Edward Holmes (15)
Landau Forte College

Writer's Block

I sat at my desk unable to write. Not knowing what to describe, incapable of putting pen to paper. So many ideas and stories unwritten. Endless things to write about but not enough words to explain their meanings. Unaccountable feelings and emotions that need describing, but I can't … writer's block.

Adam Mangnall (14)
Landau Forte College

Waiting In The Dark

I lay shivering in the dark, awaiting the dreaded noise. Rolling over to the next image, I found the old memory of better times. People laughing, who now lay silent. Children playing, toys now gone. I lay waiting, waiting for the noise of the overhead drone. Waiting in the dark.

Fiona Rudge (15)
Landau Forte College

Torn

I looked in the mirror, I was black and blue. *How could he have done this?* I thought. I had had a hard life and now was no exception. I had to get out. Get out, as far away as possible. *Bang!* That was it, he's back. Now what?

Tamika Short (15)
Landau Forte College

Ariel

An angel? No! A spirit! A girl? No! A boy? No! An it! And Prospero treats her, I mean it, like a slave. But why? What has Ariel ever done to Prospero except serve him faithfully? Not a friend, a slave. Nothing but a slave.

Aniessa Windridge (12)
Landau Forte College

Abuse

'Ouch!' She hit again! She locked me in the bathroom with a bucket full of poisonous liquids. I nearly died that time but that is one of Mum's games we play every night! She starves me! I hate her! I hate her! Someone save me! Anyone, please.

Sophie Middleton (12)
Landau Forte College

Caught

He stayed in the shadows, slowly creeping, unseen
by unsuspecting 'victims'. Then he came into view
and ran at me. I tried to run but I was pulled back
by some force and I blacked out. That day I swore I
would become a ninja and make that person pay.

Oliver King (12)
Landau Forte College

Sarah Scared

Lightning thrashed around the room. Memories clashed together in my mind. I was a girl again, being chased, laughing on the beach, by Callum. I was fourteen, running hard, my heart pounding like drums. Hot tears pouring down my shivering cheeks. Then I woke … without Callum. With fear again.

Ariel Draper (12)
Landau Forte College

The Chase!

He leapt on the boat, hurling the anchor into the deep blue sea! A gush of air flapped his rosy cheeks back and forth. The sounds grew louder, echoing from the distance. Finally he reached the shore, his feet sank into the golden sand, sweat trickling from his brow.

Ashleigh Harrison (12)
Landau Forte College

The Chase

I could sense my tormenter as sweat was trickling down my face. I had little chance of survival. They were going to find me and kill me. My only way out was to jump. It was steep but I risked it. I was falling

...

Omar Iqbal (17)
Landau Forte College

169

Embarrassing Moments

Laughing, sniggering, pointing. The day I dressed wrong. Walking through the halls, everyone stared. What was so wrong? All day I had funny looks. It wasn't my fault. Trousers on my head, T-shirt on my legs, socks on my arms. This couldn't be right. Why did I have everything wrong?

Emily Harrison (16)
Landau Forte College

Exaggeration

Who could perpetrate such a heinous crime? The initial shock, that sense of bereavement, the tears. An insidious invader has ruined my life. The forces are against me. I know I've been told a million times not to exaggerate but really, this is ridiculous. Where on Earth is my lunch?

Adam Bowler (17)
Landau Forte College

171

My Ode To Rambling

When confronted with a problem such as this, it is often better to write the first thing that comes to one's mind. However, this can frequently result in a very long and meandering story that is about as entertaining as the task that sits before me. Thank you for listening.

Richard Unwin (17)
Landau Forte College

My Security

It was snowing. I ran through the wood. I tripped. I fell. Coldness seeped in. Going to die. Alone. Silence. Darkness. Suddenly, a feeling. Warmth, a touch, his touch. Pulling me. Carrying me, cradling me. To safety, his safety, my security. Save me! Hold me! Love me.

Scarlett O'Hagan (17)
Landau Forte College

Crash

He loved her, and she loved him, so it seemed.
They'd been together since school.
One summer morning travelling on a long country
road, the car lost control and they ended in a ditch.
Together they died that night. They never even had a
chance to make up!

Natalie Clarke (15)
Landau Forte College

Untitled

I was eating my breakfast when she came in with a bruised face, tears rolling down her cheeks. I knew what was wrong. It had happened before but this was the last straw. I charged upstairs and grabbed my shotgun. I smashed down their door and shot him dead.

Hasaan Rehman (15)
Landau Forte College

Dark Night

The weather was torrential and the night was dark.
I let him in. He was sat beside me, he didn't say
a word and dodged every question. Suddenly he
attacked, I fought back and kicked him out of my car.
I sped away. I will never trust a stranger again!

Jayde Wright (15)
Landau Forte College

Daydream

Running away, getting faster and faster, I glance behind me, it's catching up with me. Terrified I run on, feeling out of breath, my knees nearly collapsing. So I stop the treadmill, grab my bags and walk out of the gym, until next time.

Charli Lawson (15)
Landau Forte College

Crash

The night the little girl's life got turned upside down. Her first day in Year Two and she loved every minute. Couldn't wait to tell her mum all the exciting things she'd done. Mum was late, torrential weather. Car crashed down a gutter. Mother's dead, now she's alone.

Sophie Hawker (15)
Landau Forte College

Wax

When cars break down people always end up in mysterious places.
The kids didn't realise an abandoned village was close by. The crazy men found them and they all seemed to be a little worse for wear. It was only the pretty people that survived.

Olivia Cunningham (14)
Landau Forte College

179

Blocked!

Once, late at night, I was incredibly bored. I opened up a conversation with my best friend Lindsey on MSN. She asked me how my weekend went and I typed 'Gr8'. She suddenly went offline. After checking my inbox a message appeared: *Birthday reminder Linzi-loll2*. Whoops!

Victoria Wiffison (15)
Landau Forte College

Consequences

To this day I still cannot catch my breath, and for my whole life it has felt like I was being watched. A debt is a debt, and mine is one I cannot repay. For what I took was priceless. It would have been his birthday today.

Harry Stewart (15)
Landau Forte College

Double Theft

Car stolen. Called my phone in the glovebox, begged for it back, said it was a present for the wife. Found it on my drive with two theatre tickets. Got home after the show. Door wide open, everything inside gone. A message scrawled on the mirror. *Enjoy the show?*

Gregory Palfreyman (15)
Landau Forte College

Death's Chase

The harrowing groans of Hell echoed through the lifeless city. There was no return. Survival was priority. Hope was my aid through the lonely death-filled streets. Help was coming. When Hell is full, the dead will walk the Earth. Co-operation was the key to escaping the undead creatures.

Simon Mackay (17)
Landau Forte College

Bumper To Bumper!

Twenty furious white men were gunning for the lone black man as they chased after him. The scared man swerved into corners trying his hardest to avoid contact with any of the monstrous mob. All any of them wanted was to beat the black man.
The Grand Prix ended.

Daniel Notiscie (16)
Landau Forte College

Anticipating Pain

In his intoxicated state, I felt his anger and unjustified revulsion towards me. Each night I lay quietly, praying underneath the safety of the cotton, begging God he would not enter. As light crept around the frame, I was losing faith. Another night of torture.

Joanne Wheeldon (17)

Landau Forte College

Broken Thoughts

The camera never lies, she sighs. The promise never lasted. And now she's obsessed with the mess left behind. Her heart repulses the image before her, the slow-moving pain - the bracelet left behind. Broken thoughts - she'll never trust again. Too late.

Emma King (17)
Landau Forte College

Where Is He?

I peered out of the window, he was nowhere in sight.
The relief ran through me! Nowhere near the tree
or behind! A smile spread across my face, until …
what's that? It was only the weirdo training his dog
for Britain's Got Talent! He wouldn't get through
with that act.

Alice Coupe (17)
Landau Forte College

Runaway

The man, being chased through a car park by men who were like giants. Jumping over cars, dancing around corners. He could see the gate, the gate to freedom. He sped up, hearing the giant's footsteps closing down on him. He was within inches, then *bang!* Tackled by a child.

Luke Bateman (16)
Landau Forte College

Discovery

Walking by a lake. Something catches my eye. I whip round, but there's nothing, not a ripple. Carry on walking. There it is again! Hurry away, but the thing keeps following, at the edge of my vision. Turn round, nothing. Turn back. It's in front of me. Then … nothing.

Naomi Green (15)
Landau Forte College

Limbo

The red, taut and strong underneath me. As thick as my leg, lay tight. I walked across but I never fell. The people watched me, always cheered. Just then I saw fear. The composition that lay below me, bonded, guile; about to throw me. Slithered like a poisonous snake. Dead!

Caſſam McCormack (15)
Landau Forte College

Football Day

As the final whistle blows, we struggle and push through the crowds to be the first ones out the ground. The adrenaline begins to pump, we chant and they chant, we throw missiles as do they, the two packs of grown men meet and the battle begins.

Grant Houldsworth (15)
Landau Forte College

Icy Incidents

Hot sand burns underfoot. She kneels, sobs. The passion inside her heart streams out through salted drops. Life is now an empty void. Her twin - herself, gone. Forever. She grasps the blade of steel and implements it. Hot blood, hot tears, on hot ground. Brother appears around the corner. Screams.

Fleur Archer (14)
Landau Forte College

Great Storm

The ship rolls as it falls into the wave trough. Spray bursts over the bow, flattened into a veil by the mournful gusts. A short voyage, now a fierce battle against the winds and waters. The mast strains. The keel lifts. Finally: capsized. The model boat rests, pathetic and unreactive.

Matthew Arran (15)
Landau Forte College

Custody

I thought I heard her shout. I ran upstairs as the shutters pounded against the open window. I opened her door - she was gone. My heart began to race as tears streamed down my face. I ran to the window as he drove away. He'd found us, it was over.

Hannah Nichols-Green (15)
Landau Forte College

Catch Me If You Can

I looked down in anguish, the blades of grass stinging my legs as I ran faster and faster. Beads of sweat raced down my forehead as I heard heavy footsteps thudding behind me, getting louder and closer. My heartbeat thundered in my chest as I pelted past the winning line!

Samantha Charles (15)
Landau Forte College

Hiding

He ran as fast as his legs could carry him. Faster and faster, feet plunging into the water-logged ground. Gnarled trees surrounded him. His eyes scanned the surroundings searching for somewhere to hide. He stood up. Screeched. Looked down. There on his arm a splodge of bright orange paint.

Cadell Barker (15)
Landau Forte College

Butterflies

Sweat dripped from my petrified face, hands shaking, so scared of what was to come next. Slowly and slowly getting closer to the most terrifying thing I had ever seen. A tear, another rip, rip, rip! There they were. The most amazing yet horrifying exam results ever to be seen.

Rachel Saul (15)
Landau Forte College

Into The Abyss

Huskies pull me across the never-ending fields of ice,
the Arctic wind sweeps across my face. The weight
of my sledge pushes against the ever-weakening ice.
I hear a crack. I cut the reins to free the huskies from
my inevitable peril and bring my journey to an end.

Oliver Ridfey (15)
Landau Forte College

Morning

I woke up early that morning, the wind was clattering against the shoddy glass panes, it was howling like a lost wolf and the dogs were barking like savage beasts. I got up, charged down the corridor, hopped in the shower, the water pierced my back like shards of ice.

Biffy Gadsby (14)
Landau Forte College

Was It Dad?

I finally arrived home, Mum lay crouched on the floor with tears running down her face. Dad came in with an angry expression on his face walking up and down the kitchen, Libby was screaming. There was silence. 'What's happened?' Mum had a bruise on her face, was it Dad?

Rosie Simpson (12)
Landau Forte College

The Miracle

She came home today. The day before had been a disaster, half of her party were gone forever. We knew they would not come back. They hadn't said that Iraq would be like this and we all thought that it was a miracle. She had survived.

Lieselotte Aberg (12)
Landau Forte College

Your Blood, The Key

'When the wind howls do not scream. They will hear you. When the owls screech at you, do not move.' 'But why, Mother, why must we run away?' the girl stuttered with tears streaming down her cheeks. 'Because the evil is coming, the evil wants your pure blood, Mary.'

Lauren Coffings (12)
Landau Forte College

Empty Lane

The lane was closed, there was a man crawling out of the bushes, he was hurt, his head was half on, half off, he was covered in blood. Then he said, 'Argghh! Help me please!' then he fell to the floor with a bullet in the centre of his forehead!

Alex Moir (12)
Landau Forte College

The Boy Whose Parents Loved Him

The boy who lived in the countryside came home from university. He wanted to give his parents a big surprise. At the door he found his family cold and cheerless to support him with his studies. His parents sold all their cattle and led a very poor and simple life.

Amy-Marie Reeves Foster (12)

Landau Forte College

204

Fear . . .

He walks towards the headmaster's door. Everyone looks and feels his fear. He looks down at the cloth covering the item that he does not even know. He enters the room … He takes the cloth off the item. A sigh of relief is heard as he looks at the apple.

Terri-Ann Palmer (12)
Landau Forte College

Will This Ever Stop?

I was happy. We were happy until … One day when I came home, he was angry again. I tried to get help, I really did! But it was too late I ran into my room and locked the door. He was shouting my name, will this ever stop?

Emily Stokes (12)
Landau Forte College

Gone

It has sunk in now. He is gone. I may not have seen him in a long time but I always had him in my head and heart. I have a picture of him on my desk. He does know I love him, doesn't he?

Nathan Robinson (13)
Landau Forte College

The Flight

My first time on a plane. Luggage ready and on the plane. Showing the passport, going through check in. Boarding the plane. Take off soon. Clearance for take off. Fins; check, engines; check. Ten, nine, eight, seven, six, five, four, three, two, one and ... 'Wake up, school in five minutes.'

Alex Withey (13)
Landau Forte College

Bang

Bang! Go the guns that will kill us, I may never see my family again. Only the lucky ones will survive. My stepbrothers are out there. I have three. *Bang! Bang! Bang!* Oh God, no, they're all dead. Now it's my turn to go, here we go. *Bang!*

Scott Gregson (13)
Landau Forte College

209

Into The Star-Spangled Night

Clambering onto the scaly back of the vast dragon, it feels like a blurred dream. My fingers ripple across the shimmering, yet icy cold scales and I feel like I'm about to burst with nerves. It's not long before we're flying. Off into the raven-black sky, illuminated by stars.

Alexandra Duesbury (12)
Landau Forte College

It

I was alone in the girls' changing room after the try-outs for soccer. When I heard something shake, nothing could be seen. Then a locker burst open. I spun around, out sprawled a green slimy thing. Automatically I shot up and backed away. Obviously I screamed, but it ran off.

Kelly Harland (12)
Landau Forte College

Me And My Princess

One morning in the middle of the day I heard a beautiful sound. I sat listening, it was coming from the village. That night I heard it again, I followed it and that is how I found my bride.

Sharna Farrar (12)
Landau Forte College

212

Life As A Hero

The house was empty. There was no furniture, no electricity, nothing. Suddenly a giant sea serpent arose from the lake. I pulled out my sword and jumped up. I thrust my sword into the monster's heart. It recoiled back into the lake and died. I was welcomed as a hero.

Andrew Mould (12)
Landau Forte College

Night Out!

At a house my friends and I upstairs, parents down.
That's when it happened. We heard a creak on the
stairs, expected nothing. I thought it was Mum and
Dad. Wrong! We went downstairs. Two people
sitting in my parents' chairs. Headless! Gruesome!
Still in house?

Zoe Taylor (12)

Mortimer Wilson School

214

End Of Life

There I was at the end of my life. This mental man
was shadowing me with a dagger. One minute I was
standing, the next dead. Blood was squelching out
of me, he dragged me out to the petrified woods.
Buried me down deep with the weapon in my heart.

Lauren Coffedge (12)

Mortimer Wilson School

The End?

'Help!' I screamed. I was trapped in the boot of a strange man's car.

'Just be quiet. You'll live,' shouted the man, trying to shout over the radio speakers. We travelled 60mph down the back streets (30mph over the limit).

'Where you taking me?' We were heading towards the canal!

Zak Heywood (11)
Mortimer Wilson School

Untitled

It is dark. I am breathing heavily. They are going to find me. I could hide forever, they'll get me. If they do … I'm dead! If I find them … I'm dead! If I make a sound … I'm dead! If I do anything I'm dead. I wake up and live again.

Shaun Johnson (12)
Mortimer Wilson School

217

Untitled

Slumped in class, nothing to do so I gossiped to my mates then the teacher saw me and moved me to the back. Now what was I supposed to do? No mates, I couldn't do anything, so bored. That's when the table went over, not bored then!

Jasmine Barker (12)
Mortimer Wilson School

Aliens

A spaceship fell to England. A slimy monster came sliding out. It attacked me and wounded me but I can never die and wouldn't give up without a fight. I fought the alien single-handedly and defeated it. I had won the battle for the planet. Is it the end?

Thomas Bexton (12)
Mortimer Wilson School

The Ghost

Standing alone. The shadow of an old castle surrounded by melting snow and ice. Looking up I saw a ghostly young child. It stood, staring into nothingness. Running into the castle, it seemed like I had been chasing for a lifetime. Sudden darkness. Then I was at the window. Staring.

Luke Mercer (12)
Mortimer Wilson School

Untitled

Alone in the cemetery, these noises, I could hear them, but couldn't understand them, twooting, howling. The ground shook repeatedly, once, twice, three times, then the mummy returned. Out of the holy church came this ear-piercing screech, throwing me to the ground. The graveyard was awakening.

Cassandra Swanwick (11)
Mortimer Wilson School

The Paddy

Slumped in history. Work so boring. 'Sir, I'm stuck!'
'The sheet,' grumpy teacher replied. The table
lonely, cold. People had finished. I'd had enough, I
read it like he said. All I could see was 'Dan loves
Jan.' I copied. He shouted. I had a paddy.

Alice Moss (12)
Mortimer Wilson School

Sleepwalking

Asleep. *Bump, thump, clump.* Awake, *bump, thump, clump.* Look round. Dinobot's tail twitching. My tail, pinning it down. Asleep again, *bump, thump, clump.* It's outside! Get up, walk to door. Open door ... It's Optimus! Sleepwalking! Close door, grin, smile evilly, grin evilly. Embarrass him. Morning? Good. Going back to sleep.

Johannah Cooke (12)
Mortimer Wilson School

Darkness

I knew someone was following me, but I carried on. I looked frantically around me searching for someone, something, the trees seemed to swirl around me and the ground seemed to shake. Then a voice, quieter than a gentle breeze, whispered softly, 'I've got you!' Darkness, that's all I remembered.

Michael Waters (13)
St Joseph's College, Stoke-on-Trent

The Hillsborough Disaster In 1989

That city once filled with happy times, but after that event all we hear is the ringing of the chimes. In the distance the sun begins to set, on this day, we will never forget. All we feel is the presence of ghosts. We miss all those we love most.

Eleanor Seabra (12)
St Joseph's College, Stoke-on-Trent

We Are Not Amused!

'We are not amused!'
Old Queen Victoria, a plump, dumpy woman, had ordered a motorbike on a silver platter. The poor fairy godmother, ruffled and tired, had conjured up a fluorescent pink quad - her fifty-seventh try. Fairy whispered in a squeaky squeal. 'I am not amused, I give up!'

Jasmine Joynson (11)
St Joseph's College, Stoke-on-Trent

His Finger And Mine

All I saw was flashing lights. Smoke inhaled in my throat. Sitting on a rock on somewhere called Jupiter. Green skin, three fingers stuck together and seven revolting toes.
I made eye contact. He tried to lift one of his fingers. His finger touched mine. Who was he? Why me?

Jasmin Sangha (11)
St Joseph's College, Stoke-on-Trent

227

Murder

He came up the stairs.
'Hello?' said the man in the hall. 'Who … Who are you?'
No answer.
'Get out of my house!'
'No.'
'Why are you here?'
'I'm here for you!'
He saw the man take the gun out. 'Please … have mercy!'
His wife came up, they were doomed.

Michał Zurąwski (12)
St Joseph's College, Stoke-on-Trent

Weird Dream

I heard a rumbling sound, nearby round a corner,
I went and looked and it was a monkey driving a
lawnmower. I tried to run away but it caught up with
me and ran me over. I woke up screaming, it was all
a dream.

Matt Webb (12)
St Joseph's College, Stoke-on-Trent

The Kraken

Corpses of a thousand men, a million sharp teeth.
Breath of a century of dragging ships down to the
abyss. An unstoppable monster, the Kraken. Can you
imagine the last thing you see on God's green Earth
is the stench and roar of the Kraken? Living is not an
option.

Kieran Waters (12)
St Joseph's College, Stoke-on-Trent

230

She Was Gone

Sweeping around the house, my daughter was playing on the computer happily. I went downstairs, someone pulled up outside, slammed the door, I heard a scream, a shot, a loud crash … The window was open, the room wrecked, blood splattered on the wall. She was gone.

Matthew Potter (12)
St Joseph's College, Stoke-on-Trent

The Curious Explorer

The curious explorer zipped from galaxy to galaxy meeting alien life forms who have a civilisation just like ours, but he suddenly finds out his spaceship had become a beacon for Belmont, the planet eater. He looked back on Earth oblivious to the catastrophe that he has unleashed upon Earth.

Ashley Durkin (12)
St Joseph's College, Stoke-on-Trent

Untitled

Me and my mate one day went to watch Stoke, the last game of the season, Stoke losing no doubt. At half time the Stoke fans went mad swearing and drinking. Preston went mad after half time, Stoke scored two back. Hopes for next season, we would pull it back.

James Goodwin (11)
St Joseph's College, Stoke-on-Trent

Deep Water

I saw the water leaking from the door. My heart sank in fear as I moved closer and twisted the handle. Water squirted out like a tsunami, there was nothing I could do; I felt myself sinking to the bottom as my mouth filled up. I was going to die.

Georgia Murphy (13)
St Joseph's College, Stoke-on-Trent

Blaze

I edged closer to the door. I couldn't stand the heat coming from inside, but I just had to get in. I felt beads of sweat dripping down my forehead and my face being burnt a glowing red colour. Then I kicked down the door releasing the scorching flames within.

Sam Mines (13)
St Joseph's College, Stoke-on-Trent

Bryan The Snail

Bryan the snail went on holiday and had a lovely time. When he arrived back to his little snail house, all his stuff was stolen, so he was sad. He went for a walk but was squashed. His friends had a funeral for him. Bryan the snail's life had ended.

Lizzy Divers (13)
St Joseph's College, Stoke-on-Trent

Man, Machine And Doughnut

Gervis the fat accountant was at work one day when he needed to photocopy a spreadsheet. As he placed his spreadsheet under the press he began to dream of hot swirly doughnuts. He could particularly feel the heat of it in his hand. Quite obviously Gervis was photocopying his hand!

Luca Gilardenghi (13)
St Joseph's College, Stoke-on-Trent

237

Brother

Six schools in four years! I never fit in. I play the
keno, the idiot … Anything!
One sinister night a light filtered through my window.
I was sucked into a metallic spacecraft, creatures
crowded around me. 'Don't hurt me,' I whimpered.
'We won't,' rasped the 'Brother'.

Isaac Campbell (12)
St Joseph's College, Stoke-on-Trent

Magic Spoon Child

And they all died … unfortunate … Isn't it … Their parents were devastated and so were the cattle, the firemen let the flames burn as the evil devil child went in with a magic spoon, and the building burned to dust except the evil devil child and his spoon …

Christopher Golik (13)
St Joseph's College, Stoke-on-Trent

A Moment Too Late

I stood there in shock and disbelief. I pinched myself. This couldn't be happening. The whole neighbourhood went up in vicious flames. I had no choice, I had to go back. I ran frantically towards the chaos, but the heat proved too much. I was too late. She was dead ...

Emily Cope (13)
St Joseph's College, Stoke-on-Trent

In The Street

I was so nervous watching my step, you could see I was wobbling. My heart was pounding. Suddenly! I was stuck. I tried to pull myself out, but I was stuck. There I stood standing in the street. My high heel was trapped in the middle of the pavement.

Hannah Shepka (13)
St Joseph's College, Stoke-on-Trent

Lonely Eyes

I had him once and I let him go. As a cop you can never live with yourself, especially with six others dead but, restraining him again, I looked into his serial-killer eyes. I asked … but he stopped me and said, 'Not serial … Lonely.'

Jonathan Maskrey (13)
St Joseph's College, Stoke-on-Trent

The Darkness

It was a dark, dark night. In the midst of the wood, he was travelling by horseback. The horse collapsed to the floor. There was a bright light in the distance. Then, there was darkness.

Edward Thompson (12)
St Joseph's College, Stoke-on-Trent

243

A Life Of Lies

I always knew my life was too good to be true. I had loving parents, and got everything I wanted. But that's all ruined now. I heard them talking, 'I think she's old enough to know.'
'Old enough to find out she's adopted.'
I fell to the floor. *Adopted?*

Emily Lloyd (13)
St Joseph's College, Stoke-on-Trent

Puzzle

I sprinted through the narrow, bloody corridors. My throat was tightening from the thick, sickening air I was breathing in. Was there a way out? It was like I was trapped in a dark damp cellar with no way out. I shouted as loud as ever, but no one heard.

Grace Wilson (13)
St Joseph's College, Stoke-on-Trent

Mindless Fight

'Ouch, ow, stop it.'
'Sorry, ow, why did you punch me?'
'Oww! Eye!'
'Sorry.'
'Clever aren't you?'
'Ow, ow, ow.'
'I'm telling.'
'You pushed me down, I'm gonna kill you mate.'
'Too late I've won the round of that.'

Abby Whitehurst (13)
St Joseph's College, Stoke-on-Trent

Invasion

Breathing, heavy, not human, more than one
heartbeat, whatever they are, they will find us soon.
Then we will have to fight, just 13 years old and we'll
have to kill. I check the standard school air rifle, wait,
the breathing's stopped. I load my gun and look up.
Bang …

Ryan Getley (13)
St Joseph's College, Stoke-on-Trent

The Walk Up To My Piano Lesson

Nearing the death-black gates a gust of freezing wind hit me. The gates opened and I crept up the driveway to the manor. I stopped at the enormous oak front door, my hands shaking as I reached for the knocker, tears gushed down my face, my heart pounding ...

Tom Attwood (13)
St Joseph's College, Stoke-on-Trent

Unexpected

Alone on the train, travelling, looking out of the window, it's gloomy. Sighing, she arrives, no idea what will happen. Walking the streets, there's no crowd. A sound breaks the silence, she turns and gets slammed against the bricks. Lying there, beaten. That empty, silent night she was mugged.

Zenab Issa (13)
St Joseph's College, Stoke-on-Trent

The Door

It was silent, nobody could be heard as I emerged closer and closer to the black and white door. The door had cobwebs hanging like baskets and it smelt like gone-off fish. I opened the door, was this to be the end of a short, short journey?

Ronan Evans (14)
St Joseph's College, Stoke-on-Trent

The Deathly Forest

The dark, dingy, deathly forest. Wolves howling and bats flying and flapping as forceful as a door being forced open! The trees hanging over like shadows and the winding, whispering walk along the path. Do you dare to take the risk? Do you want to walk the walk?

Laura Clarke (14)
St Joseph's College, Stoke-on-Trent

The Ice Cream

One day, a little girl found an ice cream in her room. She couldn't believe it, her first ice cream! She was so excited! She walked over to her ice cream. She carefully picked it up and went to lick it. Great! Hard plastic touched her tongue! She sighed, annoyed.

Josie Prina (14)
St Joseph's College, Stoke-on-Trent

Trees Have Secrets

He was walking through the dark woods. He saw a bright blinding light peering through the trees. He noticed there were people stuck. As the light came closer a spaceship came flying down from the sky, 'Help!' that was his last word, you can't speak inside a tree. Can you?

Hayley Caton (14)
St Joseph's College, Stoke-on-Trent

Lollipop!

A small child, the best present in the world, a big juicy lollipop! It's like your dreams have come true. So when Sally received her 99p double sugar-coated lollipop she was over the moon! Just as she licked every inch twice round, it fell, fluff covered it, dreams shattered.

Heidi Culverwell (14)
St Joseph's College, Stoke-on-Trent

Futile Fear

Eerie, muffled splutter. Warily pushing the creaky door open, I made sure I was wearing my best pugnacious look. Empty but for a wardrobe. The noise came again. Creeping forward, I clicked the catch and opened the wardrobe. But still no one. Then I saw the bottom shelf. A dictaphone!

Esther Rich (13)
St Joseph's College, Stoke-on-Trent

Our Journey

The mind-blowing space of nothingness, twinkling
tealights guide the way; as we're soaring through the
blackest black, the light blinding. Every ray. Soaring
high above the lightest of clouds, roaming free in this
magical place; sparkling lights upon blankets of black
as we float through outer space.

Rosanna Cocks (13)
St Joseph's College, Stoke-on-Trent

Funeral For A Friend

The dark crows swooped down over the empty grave of J R Turner who was scheduled a funeral. I was digging with Tom, when we started fighting. I tried to stop him when he hit me. I picked up the shovel, struck him down, realising I killed him … I ran.

Robat Jones (14)
St Joseph's College, Stoke-on-Trent

Head Pains

He woke up with a stabbing pain. 'Ow! I need to take some pills.' He went downstairs to take some painkillers. 'That's better.'
He got changed, had some breakfast and strutted out the front. People were staring. 'You've been stabbed in the head,' screamed someone. Suddenly he dropped down, dead.

Qasim Hussain (14)
St Joseph's College, Stoke-on-Trent

The Dark Room

A man staggered towards a blank wall, a dim light on the roof. The man held out his hands. He continued to walk, the lights flickered vigorously , unlit figures raced around him. The lights relit. The man stared at the wall, it read: *You are not alone.*

Cam Finney (14)
St Joseph's College, Stoke-on-Trent

Dying

I looked around, it was black, I couldn't see. I was scared, the nervous energy pulsating through my veins. I turned around, still black, as mysterious as a dark alley. Was this the end? Would I die petrified? This wasn't how I pictured dying, but this was how I'd die.

Ed Goacher (14)
St Joseph's College, Stoke-on-Trent

Round Pound

Once upon a time I was walking on a mound then
I saw a round pound that bounced on the ground.
That beautiful sound of the pound on the ground. I
picked up this pound that I found on the ground and
bought a hound with this magical round pound.

Libby Adnams (14)
St Joseph's College, Stoke-on-Trent

The Lady And The Sunglasses

'Buy me, lady!' a little voice whispered from behind the straw hat rack.
'Strange, I didn't know that hat racks could talk,' said the lady searching through hanging straw shapes.
'I can see!'
As she reached the back a beautiful pair of sunglasses emerged. They lived happily ever after.

Jessica Evans (14)
St Joseph's College, Stoke-on-Trent

Perry Dobar

Perry Dobar sat up a tree. Perry Dobar cut his knee. What could he lose on an old summer snooze, until he fell out of the tree. Perry Dobar's mother, was so sad she could hardly blubber. When the doctors came, they all did the same. Poor old Perry Dobar.

Kathryn Scott (13)
St Joseph's College, Stoke-on-Trent

Corridor Of Terror

I woke up startled by the midday sunlight fiercely shining through the half-open blinds. I couldn't hear anything, it was as if time had come to a stop. Suddenly sound flooded into my ears and the corridor outside my room filled with screams of terror. Then … silence again. Silence.

Arthur Muffee (13)
St Joseph's College, Stoke-on-Trent

The Beach Shore

He came out of the sea and ran to the hut, he made a hot chocolate and sat down beside one of the windows. He looked out across the bay as the waves crashed in on the seashore and the sun started to set. 'Nothing could beat this now.'

Miles Bloor (12)

St Joseph's College, Stoke-on-Trent

Midnight Murder

I shuffled down the silent country lane carefully
examining my past, I strided another few steps
through the deep mud, I paused. I listened for what
I thought I had just heard. I glanced into the cold
bushes and wondered. I turned. Rustling! Then my
heart beat its last beat.

Christopher Williams (12)
St Joseph's College, Stoke-on-Trent

266

Confused

We see it coming. I have a flashback. My whole life flashes in front of my eyes. We slam on the brakes. We are wearing seatbelts. He isn't. He flies. The window smashes. He wakes up. Bright light everywhere. Is he in Heaven or is he in hospital?

Zaheer Raffeeq (13)
St Joseph's College, Stoke-on-Trent

Always Following But Never There

As I pace down the path, trees beside me swaying in the wind, the breeze howling, leaves blowing in my face. I know he's watching me, following my every step. I turn to see, no one's there. I see him in the corner of my eye. I turn, no one.

Philippa Read (13)
St Joseph's College, Stoke-on-Trent

The Intrepid Explorer

He swims through the dark murky waters, he's the king of the sea. None can swim with his agility, or fight with his strength. The intrepid explorer hasn't yet lost a confrontation as he prowls his midnight turf … until … his face turns red, his sheets are wet. What's that smell?

Joseph Amef (12)
St Joseph's College, Stoke-on-Trent

The Chase For His Life

He runs from it. He doesn't know or care what it is. He doesn't look back. It's close. He loads his gun with silver bullets. He puts a wreath of garlic round his neck, cleanses his soul and is ready for the battle for his life.

Jim Read (13)

St Joseph's College, Stoke-on-Trent

The Calling Of The Spirits

It was a cold night, it was snowing outside. I stumbled into the B&B where I had arranged to meet some friends. We were going to try and contact the spirits. So there we were sitting around a table awaiting a message. Suddenly the lights went off, 'Death, beware!' *Silence*.

Sarah Bridges (13)
St Joseph's College, Stoke-on-Trent

271

The Evil Angel!

A girl called Leanne seemed innocent but she is evil. When you are least expecting her she will sneak behind you and kill you. One day she killed her sister and buried her under her own bed. Her sister haunted her and she mysteriously disappeared, never to be seen again.

Jasmine Massey (13)
St Joseph's College, Stoke-on-Trent

A Hidden Beauty

Her beauty was of that only known in fairy tales, but the world never saw her sparkling eyes. She hid in her tower and looked in a mirror, but the vision that she saw was ugly, vile. A tear crept down her elegant face and slowly turned into a waterfall.

Anna Ryder (13)
Woodlands Community School

The Garden Dog

I walked downstairs looking for my dog. He wasn't in the kitchen or the lounge. I went into the garden and Taz wasn't moving. I went up to him and he had three holes in his stomach. I turned round and my mum was holding a pitchfork.

Sam Townsend (14)
Woodlands Community School

274

Run For Your Life

The door clicked open. The cold night air spilled in. It was now or never for Mike. He sprinted, the hole loomed ever closer, he dived through it landing softly in the snow. Voices shouted behind him, but he was already gone … or so he thought, the gun fired. Death!

Ryan Thompson (14)
Woodlands Community School

Alone

I walked from my apartment towards the shops. I was alone. The shop down my road was five minutes away. The road was dark. I only heard a distant bark of a dog. I was alone. Once I was done I walked down an alley. Now I was not alone.

Harry Hampson (13)
Woodlands Community School

Him

I could hear a voice screaming my name. It got louder and louder. I got closer. I still couldn't see anyone. I could hear footsteps coming closer and closer. Who was it? He said my name once more. Then I could see him, stood there. Tears shed from my eyes.

Leane Bailey (14)
Woodlands Community School

Lost In A Daze

It jumped out of the water, its eyes beaming with rage. Ellie sat there, not a care in the world. She dangled her feet in the water, lost in a daze. Ellie began humming a sweet delicate tune. It was like silk through my ears, and then she was gone.

Stephanie Maidstone (14)
Woodlands Community School

Cold Breath

I wriggled and tried to set my hands free from the thick rope that bound them, I tried to kick out but the rope around my ankles was tied around the chair that I was sitting on. I stopped suddenly, because I felt his cold, hard breath and then darkness.

James Beardmore (13)
Woodlands Community School

279

Hostile Territory

I'm lucky to be alive. When I was in the RAF I went on a parachute mission. As I attempted jumping, the red jump light shone. I slipped and fell out of the plane. I landed somewhere in Bosnia. I had to get to an RAF air base to survive.

William Padgham (14)
Woodlands Community School

The Vampire

He floated through the window, in the form of mist. He materialized at the foot of the woman's bed, then glided to her side. She breathed softly, her hair was like soft gold. Her neck was white, like porcelain. He leant down and bit her, draining her of her life.

Ysabel Davis (14)
Woodlands Community School

Pursuit

I wiped the sweat from my brow. I kept on sprinting down the hill, taking leaping bounds. I fell. Lay broken in the mud. The hooded man, the red eyes, was still approaching. I waited for the end. He stopped next to me. He stood there, and did nothing.

Scott Vinay (14)
Woodlands Community School

Left Alone!

She knelt down onto her knees, whilst he lay there pale and white, his whole body frozen still and weak. The rain poured down, running down their faces. She held him closer. 'I love you, don't leave me!' she cried. 'I'm sorry.' Then he was gone; she was left heartbroken.

Laura Eaton (14)
Woodlands Community School

Enough

She could take it no more, being constantly told she was fat, ugly and pathetic. She wanted it to end. She was tired of crying herself to sleep every night, tired of not being the real her. She stood on the edge and closed her eyes. She had given up.

Katie Oliver (14)
Woodlands Community School

Playing Chicken

'Go you chicken, trust me you won't get hurt!' I shouted. Joe ran out, he dodged one car, the horn sounded loudly. He dodged car after car until he reached five.

'Your turn.' he said, exhausted.

I stepped out, dodged a car, stopped and waited, then *Bang!* Everything went black.

Murray Calder (14)

Woodlands Community School

Burning Mountain

The ground began to shake and rain started to fall. It wasn't rain though, it was black and when it reached the ground it stayed the same. The mountain was burning. The fire was spreading, rolling down the hill. It was time. People began to run from their houses.

Charlotte Edwards (14)

Woodlands Community School

Chain
Letter - Liberation

The letter came in the post, without warning,
without a sound. I knew what it was, it had liberation
on the envelope. So I left it, but it just sat there,
doing nothing, eating up the spaces around it. So I
sent it on, as it asked, liberation lives on.

Charles Penny (14)
Woodlands Community School

Switched Off

Silence. The machines were off now. Her broken body lay still on the hospital bed. It had happened so fast. A flash. A crash. Then it was gone. Only a wreckage was left. If only she hadn't had another drink. But it's so easy to say yes. Now she's gone.

Laura Ryder (13)
Woodlands Community School

The Box

I opened my eyes. Trapped, under a wooden lid.
Why was I there? What had happened to me? Where
had everyone gone? They were standing there just
a minute ago. A quick thudding on the box. Quietly.
Quickly. Over and over again. Voices, sounds of
hysterical sobbing. Then silence. Forever.

Vicky Frost (13)
Woodlands Community School

Waiting . . . ?

In her room she hid with fear, down her face dripped
a tear! Rocking back and forth. So distraught. Her
mother called, her breakfast awaited. The bus
outside. Horn beeping. Just waiting? Knowing she
couldn't go! People waiting … watching … staring …
her life, was it really worth living anymore?

Amy Nichols (14)
Woodlands Community School

290

Colwell - The Cool Kid Captain

He glimpsed left. He pivoted right. Nothing available! What could Colwell do? Spontaneously, his body and hair surged with confidence, vibrancy and determination. He was the star of the show; like a colossal piranha within a minute tank. He pulled back and fired. Where had it proceeded - Colwell never knew …

Max Colwell (13)
Woodlands Community School

Goodbye

I thought she was different, but no … yet again hopes of any real romance shattered in an instant. It was raining hard as we said the last goodbye on the doorstep. What is wrong with me? My time here is up. I'll see you on the other side. Goodbye.

Liam McNeiffy (14)

Woodlands Community School

The Cold Character

He was a shrewd evil man, uncaring, no feelings for who he destroys on his path to success. He was planning to bulldoze a village for his luxurious home. He had no family, was alone, a cold sinister face. One day his guard dropped, visiting the village, shot, dead.

Sam Swift (13)
Woodlands Community School

The Empty Blade

Panting desperately, she stumbles through the empty wilderness. 'Who are you? Who are you?' she whimpers. She glances behind herself, assessing the terrifying situation. The darkness dawns, sinister breath down her neck … She quivers to the icy ground, a 9 inch butcher's knife in her heart. The empty wilderness, empty …

Encarf Uppaf (14)

Woodlands Community School

The Carriage

The carriage lay wrecked on the hill, abandoned to the mercy of time. The wind rushed past it, running its coarse path. The corpses of the carriage's final passengers lay rotting inside it. The horrors they witnessed, lurking on that road, forgotten; but the horrors lurk on …

Henry Wilks (14)
Woodlands Community School

Over The Boundary!

'Centre please umpire,' I said in a confident voice. 'That is,' he replied. 'Right arm over player,' he stated. The bowler ran up. I repeatedly tapped my bat on the ground. He released the ball, it pitched up. I made contact, allowing it to fly over the boundary for six.

Thomas Muirhead (14)
Woodlands Community School

Currency

Wake up John! You've won a million … Shock swept
across his face. After a moment John leapt out of
bed. He bought; cars, paintings and even a house.
John arrived at the bank to discover he had nothing,
b-but I won a million … 'Yes one million yen.'

John Newbold (14)
Woodlands Community School

297

Woman In White

They met at the wedding. They danced; for a while. They walked; for a while. He told her he loved her. She told him they could never be together. He watched, by moonlight, as she glided back into the room and towards the arms of her newly-wed husband.

Sophie Haff-Luke (13)
Woodlands Community School

Utopia

Everybody has their own image of a 'perfect world'.
Some people think that the 'perfect world' has no
war, no slavery, just peace … But really the idea of
Utopia is just that, an idea and that's all it will ever
be. A world of our own just for our imaginations.

Georgina Beighton (14)
Woodlands Community School

Untitled

He came without warning from behind, she saw
glaring eyes before he struck her down and stamped
on her with his big black boots. She lay dead; rain fell
from the moonlit sky onto his rusted skin as he lay on
top of her. The door opened. The engine stopped.

Tom Marshall (14)

Woodlands Community School

Gone

Ice was melting on her pale cheeks and the stars glistened above. He kissed her gentle lips and whispered, 'I love you.' He looked into her yearning eyes. He walked away and left her standing, cold. Lonely and broken. A tear trickled down her ashen face. He was gone. Forever.

Emilie Hindle (14)
Woodlands Community School

Fashionably Late

I stared, she glided across the grass elegantly, her back glistening in the sun. She always seemed fashionably late. *I hated her!* I bent down, picked up a rock, the shadow of the rock went over her. The rock hit her, her back cracked. The snail was no more.

Jessica Biffington (14)
Woodlands Community School

The Party

It starts tonight at 7.00pm, I must look great ... who knows who will be there ... Mum said no alcohol ... stuff her ... she can't rule my life! I'll drink till I'm sick! It's 6.45, I haven't done my make-up ... I guess I'll just have to be late to the party ...

Naomi Effis (13)
Woodlands Community School

The Lake

The sun reflected off the glistening lake, they sat together happily. He looked at her, the ripples of the water danced across her soft skin, her sweet smile making him grin back, blushing red. She came closer and kissed him softly. They slept together in each other's arms, hand in hand.

Scott Griffiths (13)

Woodlands Community School

A Peter Pan Tale

Clang! went the two swords of Peter Pan and Captain Hook. It was a ferocious fight, swords blazing in the sun. Pan was backed to a corner about to fly when Hook kicked him down; Hook raised his sword ready to kill … when suddenly a voice arose, 'Tom tea's ready!'

Andrew Kay (14)
Woodlands Community School

Riot!

The noise of the crowd was deafening; 'Fight, fight …' they chanted. The circle closed in. The exhausted fighters in the centre were bruised black and blue. As the crowd clambered over each other, shouts rang out: 'Teacher!' there was a crushing stampede, leaving two exhausted figures on the ground.

Michael Holden (14)
Woodlands Community School

The Coming Future

The bright light above and cold table beneath
combined into a feeling of discomfort. I got up …
As I stood up and walked across the room I glanced
back, I was horrified with what I saw, it was me lying
on the table. Was this what was coming to me?

Curtis Harlow (14)
Woodlands Community School

Shot In The Dark

The bullet drove into my chest, penetrating my heart. I fell backwards landing on the pavement. I felt the pain rush to me, I felt the blood trickle down my stomach, it hurt. I began to see red. I felt cold. I saw a light, I followed … I was gone.

Sam Andrews (14)
Woodlands Community School

At The Pier

I stood at the end of the pier, staring at the moon. I thought about my life … what life? There was no one special in my life, and everyone hates me after what I've done … There was no point to carry on living with this hanging over me. I jumped.

Alex Preedy (14)
Woodlands Community School

Underwater

She stood, angry and crying, on the ship, but as she turned around, she saw the remains of the deck plunging into the bottomless sea. The enemies had come and gone, destroying her home. So she took one last glance above water, then held her breath, and drowned.

Genevieve Tawiah (13)
Woodlands Community School

Walk The Plank

The wind whistled against the big black sails. Jimmy stood there watching the young boy walk along the thin long plank. 'Die,' they shouted, 'you don't deserve to be on this ship!' The boy slowly walked down the plank with tears running down his face. Then he jumped … and drowned.

Megan Sharratt (13)
Woodlands Community School

Mysterious Man

I heard the doorbell ring, I knew who it was, I didn't know what to do. It rang several times, it seemed to get louder every time. My knees began to shake. My stomach began to turn. I sat on my bed. The door opened and there he was …

Charlie Greenalf (14)
Woodlands Community School

Dawn Of Death

Cries, horns, drums of war to death, honour and other things, these are the vows of a soldier. Death before dishonour was the platoon and they were at the last stand with their captain. They were saviours of that day and their names truly lasted upon the dawn of death.

Paul Rooney (13)
Woodlands Community School

The Number 50

Is 50 a word or a number? Well, it's both. '50' written as 5-0 is a number but it can be a word - fifty. Ummmm. This is confusing. This is very hard, just like 'What is the meaning of life?' and 'Why is blue, blue?' What is 50? You decide!

Leah Clifford (13)
Woodlands Community School

Time

Time goes quicker when you worry about it. So you should stop worrying about it. But you can't. 'What's the time?' 'How long now?' You don't mean to. Time will always be there. It might rush past. Can't live without it. See, now you're worrying aren't you?

Rosalyn Marshall (13)
Woodlands Community School

Stage Fright!

It is frightening, it is very tense, I am nervous. There is nothing I can do now. I am standing in the middle of the stage. Then suddenly the stage light comes on, I stop, everyone is staring at me and I am staring back. I run off the stage!

Emma Shaw (13)

Woodlands Community School

Hide-And-Seek

I turn around as the grey mist surrounds me. Trees tightly squeeze together. The sunlight can no longer be seen. I shout, 'Hello!' but the response is silence. They must be miles away by now. 'Where are you? The game's over now, you come out.'

Kate Booth (13)
Woodlands Community School

The Last Goodbye

'Please don't go,' she whispered.
'I have to,' he croaked back.
'You can stay. We can fight it.' She grabbed his hand
with desperate hope.
'Goodbye Daisy,' his final words. Her tears washed
the dirt off his skin. He was just another innocent in
this war of different worlds. 'Cut!'

Sophie Willis (13)

Woodlands Community School

318

The Shadow

The shadow stomped silently down the empty street towards the girl, yet she could feel its presence. Then the shadow raised its arm. Sweat dripping from her forehead, she turned to face it. She screamed, piercing everyone's ears. She was found saturated in pure blood with a white ghostly face.

Joseph Woods (13)
Woodlands Community School

Happy Birthday

I blow out the candles. My second birthday ends
the door is swung open. 'I'm afraid your father was
murdered in a terrible war incident, I'm sorry.' I sit
at the table just staring as my eyes fill with tears. My
toys still littering the table. The pain of war …

William Thompson (13)
Woodlands Community School

Silence

Entering the room, seeing my baby boy lying on a life support machine is just heartbreaking. But today is the day that I have to let him go, 'Are you ready?' the doctor questioned.

'Yes,' I said blankly. With that he pulled the plug out of the wall! Silence ...

Anna Johnson (13)
Woodlands Community School

This Is My Journey

My name is Phoebe and this is my journey. It was two years ago, I was kidnapped, sold as a slave, abused. But I am still here after everything, walking graciously downstairs, eyes darting, not trusting anyone … not after the trip from Hell and back that I outlived!

Alex Smith (13)
Woodlands Community School

Amber

Do you know me? I hope you don't, for your own sake. I'll poison you with disappointment. 'I hate you Amber.' My dad says that to me. I'm nothing like the precious stone; golden and beautiful. Amber; bruised and ugly. Amber; the one who faded out but never said goodbye.

Eleanor Hancock (13)
Woodlands Community School

323

The Warning

He had been following her since junction four. The van trailed in the distance. She tried to lose him in the field, but her car broke down! It wasn't him she should have been worried about, it was the psychopath in the back of the car! He was warning her.

Nickh Uppal (14)
Woodlands Community School

The End?

The bar came down, the rusty chain moved. I was going up. There was something odd about the person next to me. We fell, going up, down and round, upside down again, but with a gun against my head. *Bang!* I fell to the ground, white light surrounded me. Death?

Cathy Gater (14)
Woodlands Community School

Fame Is A Hollow Victory

He bashed the chords on the piano. It buzzed,
audience cheering, the lights beating down with
intense heat on his sweaty brow. He was no longer
nervous. Afterwards he left the stage - but he felt
something cold in his side; then it went black. He
died because he was famous.

John Howard (14)
Woodlands Community School

Just Another Day?

School was perfect today, hot weather, my favourite lessons with my favourite friends.
My mum wasn't home yet which was strange as she finished work at 1pm. I went upstairs to change out of my uniform. That's when I saw my mum dead, covered in blood … It was murder.

Kerry McGreene (14)
Woodlands Community School

327

Is It The End Of The Rider?

It was a cold rainy day, I was on my bike. I flew down
a dingy path, carefree. I dodged the bush but flew
over the wall. My arm, leg and face were bleeding.
Blood gushed down my body. I was scared, helpless,
someone touched me, 'Come with me!'

Samuel Parry (14)
Woodlands Community School

Tempus Fugit

Denny was speechless. They had been attacking the ship, Tempus Fugit, only to be shocked at the crew and ship. Everything looked millions of years old. The crew looked like withering corpses. The captain said in a weak voice, 'Tempus fugit.' Denny turned and fled, shocked at the ship's curse.

Sarah Jones (13)
Woodlands Community School

Pirate Ghost Ship

It was a cold breezy night on the pirate ghost ship.
The drunken old pirates were getting drunk on rum
while celebrating after finding the long-lost treasure
of Jewels Island, feasting and shouting, making a
mess. The party went on for hours getting quieter as
they retired to bed.

Christina Bayes (13)
Woodlands Community School

Perfect Aim

I rummaged around my cabin urgently as the sounds of drums approached my ship. I ran onto the deck to see the Spanish Armada heading towards me, the ship rocked and reached for the railings. My hand shook but I managed to light the cannon. My aim was perfect.

Joanna Gordon (13)
Woodlands Community School

331

Untitled

The waves got bigger and bigger as I sailed through the North Sea. I couldn't handle the ship on my own. Lightning struck the sails, I decided to go into the hold and let the sea take me wherever it took me but the storm just got worse and worse.

Jiff Straughan (13)

Woodlands Community School

The Fall Of Greybeard

The ship approached, we were definitely doomed. They were closing in, we were going to die. The cannons fired. We fired and their captain got hit squarely in the chest. Greybeard died. Another well-placed cannonball and their ship collapsed. The dead went to Davy Jones. We were victorious, *hooray!*

Bobby Buckley (13)
Woodlands Community School

333

Battle Of The Pirates

The ship approached and the men aboard the ship were ready for battle with the opposing pirate, Naveed from Pakistan. They had been fighting for many years, neither one winning. This one was the decider. When they engaged the battle was very bloody with many dead. Naveed Iqbal prevailed.

Henry West (13)
Woodlands Community School

The Epic Battle

The sound of swords clashing, both pirates locked in eternal struggle. One, Gingerbeard, was extremely concentrated. Long, curved nose, flaming red hair blowing in the wind. Baldy fought casually. Suddenly Gingerbeard felt an excruciating pain in his side. Looking down, he realised Baldy's telepathic mole had taken over his brain.

Harry Iffidge (13)
Woodlands Community School

Lost Treasure

The ship approached the harbour, the time had arrived. What we had all been waiting for. If we didn't get this right we would get hanged! We needed to get the treasure from the tavern, then we could go. Until we found the treasure had gone! Someone had taken it!

Elizabeth Thorley (13)
Woodlands Community School

The Thing That Took My Life

Out from the roaring flames crawled a dark and mysterious creature. It crawled closer and closer until it was only an arm's reach away. The thing spoke in a deep and distorted voice. I couldn't understand what it said. Until it took the mask off and took my life away.

Sam Garcia (11)
Woodlands Community School

The Storm

The wind was blowing and the thunder howled as the storm in full throttle devastated all that was in its path leaving nothing but rubble, death and destruction. Now that the storm has finished everything is silent. Nothing can be heard apart from falling rubble and distant thunder destroying more.

Anthony Murphy (12)
Woodlands Community School

Breakaway

The fog was thick as I laid the anchor. I could hardly see my way to the side of the ship. Davey crossed over to me with the key and the map. I lowered the rowing boat into the inky water, took Davey's hand and jumped overboard. We were free.

Georgia Woodhouse (13)
Woodlands Community School

Mad House

I sprinted through puddles, feet cold and numb, hair dripping wet and messy, but I had to get away. I couldn't stay in that mad house for another second; the shouting, hitting and screaming. Where was I going? I don't know. I just had to go and get away.

Beth Kean (12)
Woodlands Community School

Are They There?

Are they still there, following me? My body shivers as I run through cold puddles and the fast rain. Are they there or are they not. I'm running in the wrong direction from my house, why, why, why? I could stop or I could keep on running and running …

Mica Morrison (11)
Woodlands Community School

On The School Site

When I was on the back field in the distance was a scary figure, when it came closer it looked even more scary. When it took off its wig, it was … the school caretaker. He told me that he was going to scare off the kids on the school site.

Joe Morris (12)
Woodlands Community School

Terrified

She was worrying about it all day; she couldn't get it out of her head. Finally, it was the time. You could see she was scared by the sweat dripping down her forehead. She opened the door and let out a scream … She had spotted a spider and was terrified!

Jacaranda Brain (12)
Woodlands Community School

The Woman

The woman was walking slowly. It was dark; no one for miles. Then she could hear heavy breathing. It got faster and faster. She ran but was too slow. She felt something on her shoulder and screamed and screamed, but nobody replied. Nobody replied but the heavy breathing … *Bang!*

George Taylor (12)
Woodlands Community School

344

Information

We hope you have enjoyed reading this book - and that you will continue to enjoy it in the coming years.
If you like reading and writing, drop us a line or give us a call and we'll send you a free information pack. Alternatively visit our website at www.youngwriters.co.uk

Write to:
Young Writers Information,
Remus House,
Coltsfoot Drive,
Peterborough,
PE2 9JX
Tel: (01733) 890066
Email: youngwriters@forwardpress.co.uk